MONSTER HIGH™

HOPES and SCR

D0546394

The Monster High
Gory Gazette™
YOUR UHHH-LTIMATE SOURCE FOR GOSSIP

AN ORIGINAL GRAPHIC NOVEL

WRITTEN BY HEATHER NUHFER · ILLUSTRATED BY JOSH HOWARD

LITTLE, BROWN AND COMPANY
New York Boston

Special thanks to Venetia Davie, Tanya Mann, Darren Sander, Julia Phelps, Cindy Ledermann, Garrett Sander, Charnita Belcher, Sharon Woloszyk, and Andrea Isasi.
Cover art by Josh Howard
Cover design by Steve Scott
Interior inks by Josh Howard
Interior colors by Caravan Studio
Bubbles and lettering by Ching Nga Chan

Little, Brown and Company

Hachette Book Group
237 Park Avenue, New York, NY 10017
Visit our website at lb-kids.com
monsterhigh.com

Little, Brown and Company is a division of Hachette Book Group, Inc.
The Little, Brown name and logo are trademarks of Hachette Book Group, Inc.

The publisher is not responsible for websites (or their content)
that are not owned by the publisher.

First Edition: July 2014

Library of Congress Control Number: 2013946010

ISBN 978-0-316-25433-5

10 9 8 7 6 5 4 3 2 1

CW

Printed in the United States of America

TABLE OF CONTENTS

Frankie Stein

Monster Parents: Frankenstein and his bride
Age: How many days has it been?
Frankie is sparking with enthusiasm for unlife at Monster High. She may sometimes fall apart at the seams, but she is always there to lend a helping hand.

Clawdeen Wolf

Monster Parents: The Werewolves
Age: 15
Clawdeen is bold, opinionated, and fiercely loyal to her friends. She is the younger sister of Clawdia and Clawd, and she is Howleen's older sister.

Draculaura

Monster Parents: Dracula
Age: 1,600 years
Draculaura is kind, generous, and scary sweet. She is a vegetarian vampire and a hopeless romantic.

Cleo de Nile

Monster Parents: The Mummy
Age: 5,842 (give or take a few years)
An actual Egyptian princess, Cleo rules the halls of Monster High as captain of the Fear Squad. While a bit self-centered, Cleo is a true friend.

Ghoulia Yelps

Monster Parents: Zombies
Age: 16
Ghoulia may move a bit slowly, but she's the smartest ghoul at Monster High. She speaks only in Zombese, which most monsters can easily understand.

Abbey Bominable

Monster Parents: The Yeti
Age: 16
Abbey is enormously strong and as blunt as a hammer. Her words can come across as cold and harsh, but she has a warm heart.

Robecca Steam

Monster Parents: A Mad Scientist
Age: 116 years
Robecca is a scaredevil, and she loves adventure, particularly those that involve the catacombs.

Howleen Wolf

Monster Parents: The Werewolves
Age: 14
The younger sister of Clawdia, Clawd, and Clawdeen, Howleen is just trying to find her place in the pack.

*TRANSLATED FROM ZOMBESE

CLEO!

NOW EVERYONE CAN SEE IT WAS ME!

I'M RUINED!

<MAYBE NO ONE WILL SEE IT!>

<SOON IT'LL ALL BE HISTORY. I PROMISE.>

MAYBE YOU'RE RIGHT. ALL THE GREATEST GHOULS IN HISTORY HAVE HAD TO OVERCOME SOME SORT OF SCANDAL. I GUESS IT'S FINALLY MY TURN.

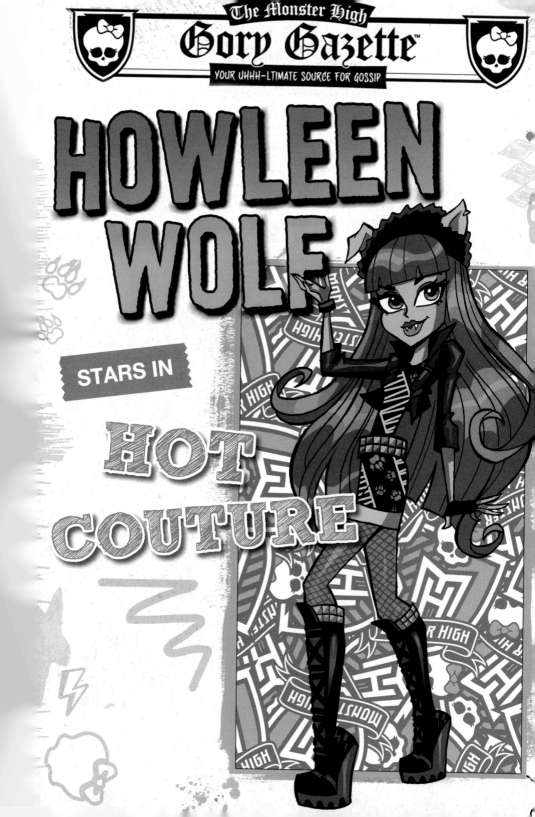

*TRANSLATED FROM ZOMBESE

GRRRR!

GASP!

WHAT HAVE I DONE?! HEATH, WE HAVE TO HIDE BEFORE CLAWDEEN SEES THIS!

MEANWHILE...

IS THERE SOMETHING ABOUT THE MOST PERFECT PYRAMID EVER MADE THAT YOU DON'T UNDERSTAND? THE PEP RALLY IS ABOUT TO START!

THE LEAD CHARACTERS, SANDY AND CHET—THEY, UH, KISS.

ME AND FRANKIE!!

OH! YEAH! RIGHT... WE'RE JUST ACTING....

WHOA. WHO'S PLAYING THE LEADS?

WELL, NO BIG DEAL. YOU'RE JUST ACTING, RIGHT?

AND IT'S NOT AS IF YOU LIKE HER OR SOMETHING.

YEAH...NOT AS IF I LIKE HER....

LATER THAT NIGHT...

DRACULAURA, YOU NEED TO GET SOME REST!

I'M ALMOST FINISHED! IT LOOKS FANGTASTIC, DOESN'T IT?

IT SCREAMS "NORMIE LIVING ROOM"!

THANK YOU!

45

WHAT HAPP—?

OH NO! ALL MY HARD WORK—GONE! THIS IS THE WORST.

HEY, GUYS AND GHOULS, WE'VE GOT A TEENY-WEENY LITTLE PROBLEM.

UM, WE DON'T THINK WE CAN DO THIS. FOR SOME REASON, I FEEL... WEIRD ABOUT DOING THE SHOW.

YEAH, WE'RE OUT!

WHAT HAPPENED TO EVERYONE? ALL OF A SUDDEN THEY SEEM SCARED TO GO ONSTAGE.

I KNOW. FOR SOME REASON, I FEEL REALLY CALM. AND I DIDN'T BEFORE.

ME TOO!

PLACES, EVERYONE!

P-P-PLACES?

I AM WANTING BADLY TO HELP OUT, BUT I AM NOT KNOWING WHAT TO GIVE. NOT MUCH NEED FOR WOOLLY MAMMOTH GROOMING TIPS.

YOWCH! YOWCH!

DON'T WORRY, ABBEY, I KNOW YOU HAVE SOMETHING ICY-COOL TO ADD!

OH...SORRY, MANNY!!

UGH! I WISH I COULD FIND THAT BOLT!

IS THAT THE THINGY YOU WERE LOOKING FOR?

MY BOLT! THANKS, ABBEY! YOU'RE A LIFESAVER!

IS NOTHING. I HAVE ALWAYS BEEN GOOD AT THE FINDING OF THE LOST THING.

AHA! I KNOW WHAT YOU CAN DO!

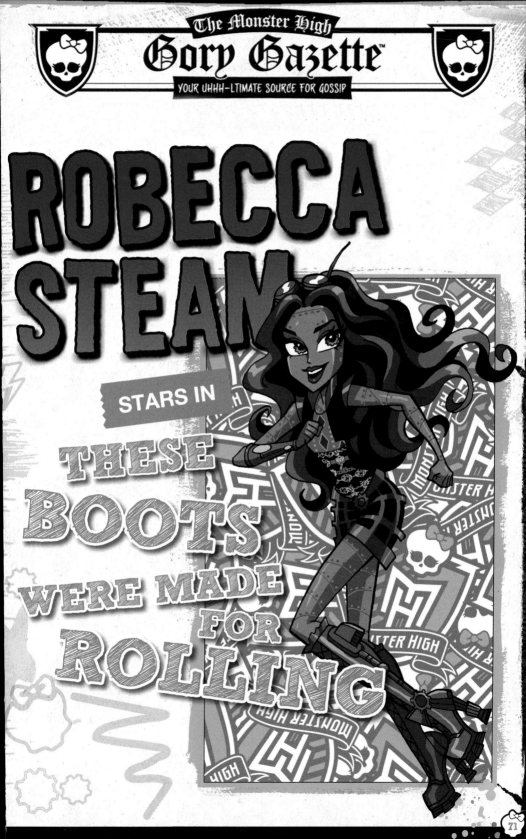

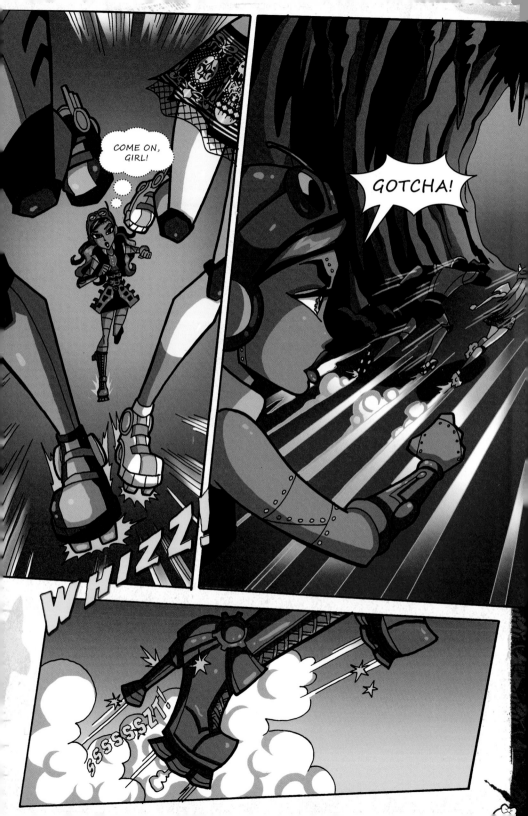

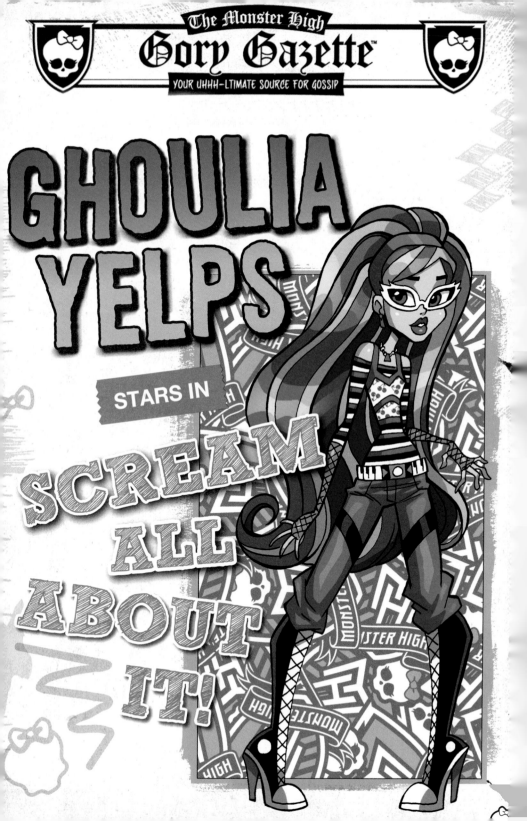

Gory Gazette Exclusive: Read a brand-new *Dead Fast* story

WORLD PREMIERE VIDEO— ALL MY MONSTERS! JUST PRESS PLAY!

▶

SCREAM!

Where there's a wolf, there's a way: Are you a fashion scream?

For more uhhh-ltimate updates,
check out gorygazette.tumblr.com

BEHIND THE SCREAMS

See how *Hopes and Screams* came to life!

Step 1: rough sketches

Step 2: inks

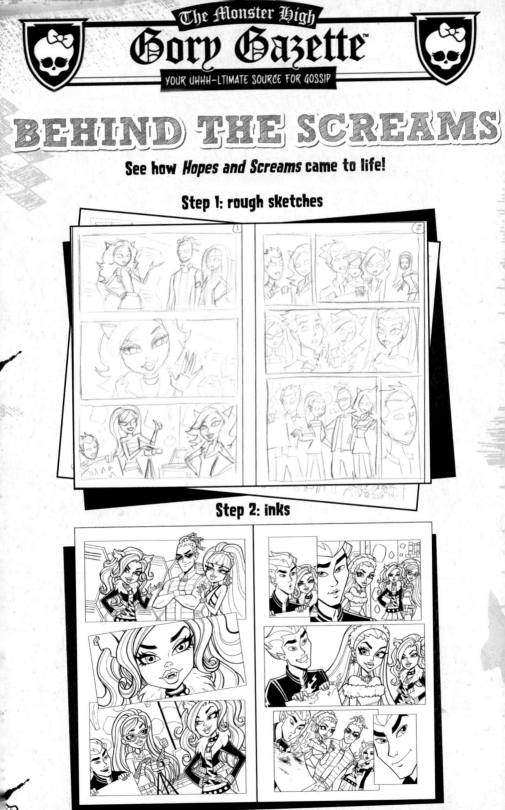

BEHIND THE SCREAMS

See how *Hopes and Screams* came to life!

Step 3: color

Step 4: balloons and text

ABOUT THE AUTHOR

HEATHER NUHFER

HEATHER NUHFER IS A SPOOKTACULAR ALL-AGES WRITER, KNOWN IN PARTICULAR FOR HER COMIC-BOOK WORK, INCLUDING THE MONSTROUSLY POPULAR *MY LITTLE PONY: FRIENDSHIP IS MAGIC*, *STRAWBERRY SHORTCAKE*, AND *THE SIMPSONS*. WHEN SHE ISN'T WRITING, HEATHER LOVES TO KNIT FREAKY-FAB SWEATERS FOR HER PUP, EINSTEIN, AND BAKE TASTY VEGETARIAN TREATS TO SHARE WITH DRACULAURA. HER BIGGEST SCREAM IS TO VISIT SCARIS!

ABOUT THE ILLUSTRATOR

JOSH HOWARD

BORN AND RAISED IN TEXAS, JOSH CAN ALWAYS BE FOUND SCRATCHING AWAY AT HIS LATEST MASTERPIECE UNDER THE LIGHT OF A FULL MOON. HE IS BEST KNOWN AS THE CREATOR OF THE COMIC BOOK *DEAD@17*, AN ACTION/HORROR SERIES ABOUT TEENAGERS, ZOMBIES, SPIRITS, AND GHOULS. (SOUND FAMILIAR?) JOSH IS MARRIED TO A BEAUTIFUL VAMPIRESS NAMED LAURA AND IS THE PROUD FATHER OF THREE LITTLE MONSTERS: LUKE, LONDON, AND WILLOW.

COMING SOON!

The next ghoulgeous Monster High graphic novel!